Fun with GRAMMAR
Book 4

ENGL.
AA

MOONSTONE

Published in Moonstone
by Rupa Publications India Pvt. Ltd 2023
7/16, Ansari Road, Daryaganj
New Delhi 110002

Sales centres:
Prayagraj Bengaluru Chennai
Hyderabad Jaipur Kathmandu
Kolkata Mumbai

P-ISBN: 978-93-5702-334-4
E-ISBN: 978-93-5702-336-8

First impression 2023

10 9 8 7 6 5 4 3 2 1

Printed in India

CONTENTS

NOUNS

Nouns *are words that name people, places, animals, things, or ideas.*

Example:

George Washington, Lata Mangeshkar (people)

New York, Mumbai (places)

Cat, Tiger (animals)

Bench, Lock (things)

Freedom, Loyalty (ideas)

Types of Nouns

Nouns are of four types as follows –

- **Common noun**

- **Proper noun**

- **Collective noun**

- **Abstract noun**

Let us discuss them one by one -

Common Noun

A common noun *is used to refer to the* general *or generic name* of person, place, animal and things.

Example:

- I am writing a **letter**.

- My **father** is cooking **food**.

Proper Noun

> A proper noun *is used to refer to a* specific *person, place or object.*

Example:

- **Delhi** is the capital of **India.**

- **Indira Gandhi** was the first female Prime Minister of **India.**

A **Is the highlighted word in the sentence a common noun or a proper noun?**

1. My father grew up in a small town. _____

2. Let me introduce you to Lata. _____

3. He is the chairman of the Indian Oil Corporation. _____

4. The books are on your table _____, _____

5. I have two cats. _____

6. Louise played with her brother. _____, _____

7. Ryan went to City Vet Pet Shop. _____, _____

8. The principal punished the mischievous boy. _____ ,

   _____

COLLECTIVE NOUNS

A collective noun *denotes a group of people or animals or things.*

Examples: fleet (group of ships), swarm (group of bees)

The **fleet** of ships carried precious cargo and passengers from distant lands.

The **herd** of cows grazed peacefully on the green grass.

Collective nouns can be treated as singular or plural.

A Complete the following sentences with a collective noun given in the box below:

choir	fleet	crowd	pack
library	swarm	bouquet	shoal

1. The _____ sang beautifully at the church.

2. The _____ of bees buzzed angrily around the hive.

ABSTRACT NOUNS

> *A noun denoting an* idea, quality, *or* state *rather than a concrete object is called an* abstract noun.

Examples: happiness, courage, danger, truth

- The sight of sunrise is **beautiful.**

- Who killed President Kennedy is a real **mystery.**

- Sometimes it takes **courage** to tell the **truth.**

- Their lives were full of **sadness.**

A **Underline all the abstract nouns from the sentences given below. First one is done for you.**

1. Lara had a <u>childhood</u> full of <u>love</u> and <u>happiness</u>.

2. The dove is a symbol of peace.

3. Mark had lot of fun in the water park.

4. I thought bees are attracted to flowers by sight and smell.

5. He takes pride in his job.

6. He cannot control his anger.

7. I had a nightmare last night.

8. Every time I hear the national anthem, my heart fills up with patriotism.

9. My grandfather is full of wisdom.

10. My manager wished me luck for my new project.

OTHER TYPES OF NOUNS

Masculine and Feminine Nouns

I am a boy. I am a male.

I am a girl. I am a female.

Is this chair a male or a female?

Masculine nouns : *These are the words which are used for men, boys and male animals, such as father and husband.*

Feminine nouns: *These are the words which are used for women, girls and female animals, such as mother and wife.*

Neuter nouns: These are the words that denote a thing that is neither male nor female such as book, pen, room, house, tree, etc.

Common- gender nouns: These are the words that can be used for both males and females such as guest.

We can change masculine nouns into feminine nouns using the following methods.

1) By a change of word. Some examples are:

MASCULINE	FEMININE
Bachelor	Spinster
Boy	Girl
Brother	Sister
Buck	Doe
Bull (Ox)	Cow
Cock	Hen
Colt	Filly
Dog	Bitch
Drone	Bee
Drake	Duck
Earl	Countess
Father	Mother
Gander	Goose

MASCULINE	FEMININE
Gentleman	Lady
Horse (Stallion)	Mare
Husband	Wife
King	Queen
Lord	Lady
Man	Woman
Nephew	Niece
Ram	Ewe
Sir	Madam (Dame)
Son	Daughter
Stag (Hart)	Hind
Uncle	Aunt
Wizard	Witch

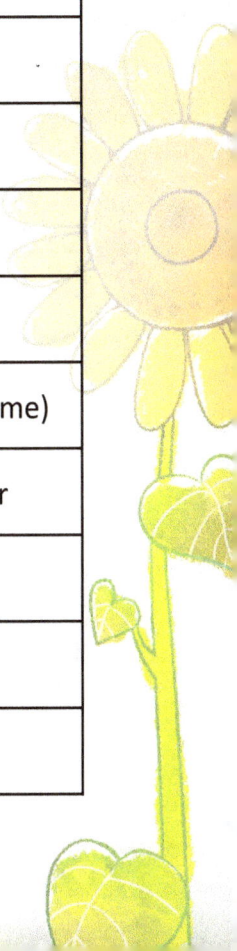

2) By adding a word . Some examples are:

MASCULINE	FEMININE
Boy friend	Girl friend (Friend is common gender)
Grand father	Grand Mother
She goat	He goat
Man servant	Maid servant
Milkman	Milk woman
Salesman	Saleswoman/ salesgirl
Washer man	Washer woman

3) By adding '-ess' to the Masculine. Some examples are:

MASCULINE	FEMININE	MASCULINE	FEMININE
Author	Authoress	Jew	Jewess
Baron	Baroness	Lion	Lioness
Count	Countess	Poet	Poetess
Headmaster	Headmistress	Priest	Priestess
Heir	Heiress	Prince	Princess
Host	Hostess	Shepherd	Shepherdess

If there happens to be a vowel letter in the last part of the masculine Noun, generally the vowel is left out and '-ess' is added to the remaining part.

MASCULINE	FEMININE
Actor	Actress
Benefactor	Benefactress
Conductor	Conductress
Enchanter	Enchantress
Hunter	Huntress

Non-Standard Formation of Feminine Nouns from Masculine Nouns through the Addition of '-ess':

MASCULINE	FEMININE
Duke	Duchess
Emperor	Empress
Master (Teacher)	Mistress
Murderer	Murderess

Without any rules:

MASCULINE	FEMININE
Groom	Bride
Fiance	Fiancee
Widower	Widow

Some Common Gender Nouns:

Baby: Male or Female	Monarch: King or Queen
Bird: Cock or Hen	Mouse: Male or Female
Calf: Bullock or Heifer	Orphan: Male or Female
Cat: Male or Female	Parent: Father or Mother
Child: Son or Daughter	Peafowl: Peacock or Peahen
Cousin: Male or Female	Person: Man or Woman
Deer: Stag or Hind	Pig: Boar or Sow
Elephant: Male or Female	Pupil: Boy or Girl
Enemy: Male or Female	Rat: Male or Female
Flirt: Man or Woman	Household Staff: Man or Woman
Foal: Cock or Hen	Sheep: Ram or Ewe

Friend: Male Or Female	Student: Male Or Female

A Write the Feminine nouns of the given words:

Masculine	Feminine
Widower	_____
Bridegroom	_____
Grand-father	_____
Salesman	_____
Dog	_____
Gander	_____
God	_____
Master	_____
Hunter	_____
Benefactor	_____
Emperor	_____
Governor	_____

When a Noun changes from Masculine to Feminine, the Pronoun in the sentence must change too.

ARTICLES

English has three articles: *A, AN,* and *THE*. These articles are used before nouns to show whether the nouns are general or specific.

The **definite article: the,** is used before a noun to indicate that the noun is known to the reader. **The indefinite articles: a an,** are used before a noun that is general or not known.

For example:

• I bought **a** blue sweater yesterday.

• I bought **an** apple and an orange. **The** apple was delicious.

A **Underline the correct article (a / an / the) in each sentence:**

1. John wanted to read a / an comic book so he went to the / a super comic store.

2. The / A church on the corner is progressive.

3. Lisa put a / an orange on her yogurt.

4. The class went on a / an field trip.

5. I borrowed an/ a pencil from your pencil box.

6. Marriam likes to read an / the short stories.

7. Monday is the/ a first day of an / the week.

8. I saw a / an elephant at the zoo.

9. Pam quickly ate the / an pizza as she was hungry.

10. The dog caught a / an stick.

B Complete the following sentences with A, AN or THE:

1. I had _____ egg and _____ glass of milk for breakfast.

2. _____ leopard which escaped from _____ zoo has been caught.

3. Have you finished reading _____ book you borrowed last week?

4. Steve has _____ terrible headache.

5. _____ event like this happens only once a year.

6. _____ rabbit was hiding in the bush. When we went near the bush, _____ rabbit ran away.

7. _____ girl you met is the class topper.

8. Can you give me _____ glass of water?

9. Who spilt ink on _____ carpet?

10. _____ oval is shaped like _____ egg.

C Complete the following sentences with A, AN or THE:

1. Danny wanted _____ new bicycle for Christmas.
   (a) A   (b) AN   (c) THE

2. Jennifer tasted _____ birthday cake her mother had made.
   (a) A   (b) AN   (c) THE

PRONOUNS

A pronoun *is a word that takes the place of a noun in a sentence.* Pronouns *are used to avoid repeating the same nouns over and over again.*

For **Example**, "Riya loves her dog".

Riya is a noun and her is a pronoun that replaces Riya's name.

Types of Pronouns

Pronouns can be divided into several categories:

personal, possessive, relative, demonstrative, interrogative, and reflexive.

Personal pronouns

Personal pronouns are always *specific* and are often used to *replace a proper noun* (someone's name) or a *collective group of people or things.*

There are two types of personal pronouns: subject and object.

When the person or thing is the subject of the sentence, **subject pronouns** *are used, such as I, you, he, she, it, we, they.*

Examples:

- I like to watch football, but he does not.

- She called him yesterday.

Object pronouns *are used when the person or thing is the object of the sentence, such as me, you, him, her, it, us, you, them.*

Examples:

- Robert trusted him with his life.

- She prepared some delicious cookies for me.

> **We** will miss the train if **you** don't wake up early in the morning.
>
> *In the above sentence, **we** is the subject of the sentence, but **you** is the object.*

A Use these pronouns to complete the sentences. You may use some pronouns more than once.

> They   he   his   she   us   she

My family consists of four people: my parents, my sister, and me.

_____ are very supportive and loving. My father works as a doctor

and _____ enjoys reading books in _____ spare time. My mother

is a teacher and _____ likes to cook delicious meals for _____.

My sister is a student and _____ loves to play the piano.

B Write the nouns that are referred to by the pronouns in bold print in the sentence in the space provided.

1. The Taj Mahal is a famous monument. **It** took several years to build.

   _____

1. Dad and I went for a morning walk. **We** walked for two kilometres.

   _____

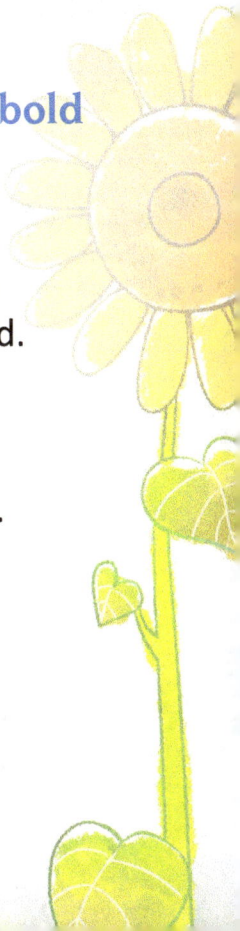

Possessive Pronouns

> Possessive pronouns *show ownership or possession of a noun such as my, our, your, his, her, its (note there is no apostrophe), their.*

Example:

- Is that **my** pen?

- No, that's **his** pen.

- The team celebrated **its** victory.

- The birds sang **their** songs in the morning.

However, there are also **independent possessive pronouns.** These pronouns refer to a previously named or understood noun. They are: mine, ours, yours, his, hers, theirs.

- That pen is **mine**.

- This car is **ours**.

- Is this book **yours**?

- I like ours better than **theirs**.

> Independent possessive pronouns are stand alone and aren't followed by any other noun.

C **Fill in each blank with the correct word from the brackets.**

1. The house belongs to the businessman. It is _____ (he, his, him).

2. The rabbits quickly ran into a burrow. Is that burrow _____ (them, their, theirs, they)?

3. Grandmother is ill. These pills are _____ (she, her, hers).

4. The church is _____ (ours, our, us). My family and I go there every Sunday.

5. Whose books are these? Are they _____ (you, yours, your)?

6. That boy is reading a book. It is _____ (me, mine, my).

7. This is John's glass. The drink is _____ (he, him, his).

8. This is Bill and Linda's dog. The pet is _____ (they, theirs, their).

Relative Pronouns

> Relative pronouns *refer to nouns mentioned previously. They are: who, whom, which, whoever, whomever, whichever, that.*

Examples:

- She is the one **who** helped me.

- The cake, **which** was chocolate, looked delicious.

- **Whichever** team wins the game will advance to the finals.

- The car **that** has a dent in the door is mine.

D **Fill in the blanks with the correct relative pronoun.**

1. Here is someone _____ you can trust fully.

2. The athlete _____ won the gold medal is from Ghana.

3. You can choose _____ you like from my team, for the task.

4. This is the place _____ I used to stay.

5. The food _____ you ordered yesterday, was not fresh.

6. The girl _____ bike was stolen was very upset.

7. This is the locker in _____ all the jewelleries are kept.

8. The movie _____ we watched last night was very scary.

9. This is the year _____ I will graduate from college.

10. I want to visit the place _____ the river originates.

Demonstrative Pronouns

Demonstrative pronouns *are used to point to something specific within a sentence. They can be singular or plural such as this, that, these, those.*

Examples:

- **This** is my friend Lance.

- **That** looks like a poisonous snake.

- The cars in the front are worth more than **those** in the back.

E Underline the demonstrative pronouns.

1. These are the books I borrowed from the library.

2. That is the house where I grew up.

3. Did you see those birds?

4. Is this pen yours?

5. Do you like these shirts?

6. That house has a kitchen garden.

7. These hotels are better than those in the valley.

8. This box is heavier than that.

Interrogative Pronouns

Interrogative pronouns *are used to ask questions. An interrogative pronoun often appears at the beginning of a question. They are who, whom, which, what, whoever, whomever, whichever, whatever.*

Interrogative pronouns **who, whose** and **whom** are used to ask questions about people.

Examples:

- **Who** is going to sing?
- **Whose** pen is this?
- **Whom** did you call just now?

Interrogative pronouns **what** and **which** are used to ask questions about living and non-living things. Sometimes **which** is used to ask about people.

Examples:

- **What** are you planning to wear tomorrow?
- **Which** of these books do you like?
- **Which** one the students got the scholarship?

F **Fill in the blanks with the correct interrogative pronouns from the box. Some words can be used more than once.**

whose	which	who	what	whom

1. _____ drove the car yesterday?

2. _____ mobile rang just now?

3. _____ is the colour of the sky?

4. _____ is the tallest building in the world?

5. _____ is in the kitchen?

6. _____ did you call yesterday?

7. _____ can be done for him?

8. _____ car is this?

Reflexive Pronouns

Reflexive pronouns *are used to show that the subject and the object of a sentence refer to the same person or thing. These pronouns end in -self or -selves. They are myself, yourself, , himself, herself, itself, ourselves, yourselves, themselves.*

Examples:

- I told **myself** to study hard for the exam.

- Lata looked at **herself** in the mirror.

- We gave **ourselves** a treat after the match.

- They bought **themselves** a new house.

G Fill in the blanks with a suitable reflexive pronoun.

1. She made the presentation _____ before the meeting started.

2. We wash the dishes _____ after dinner.

3. The cat licked _____ clean.

4. "Believe in _____". My mother told me.

5. He managed the project _____.

6. I repaired the leaking pipe in the kitchen _____.

7. She taught _____ how to play the piano.

8. We trained _____ for the tournament.

9. The newly wed couple gave _____ a holiday in Britain.

10. She made _____ a cup of tea.

ADJECTIVES

> **An** adjective is a *describing word*. **It is used to** *describe people, place* **or** *things*.

Descriptive adjectives tell us more about the size, shape, colour, texture and condition of a noun.

Example:

- I don't like **yellow** shirt.
- That is a **big** house.
- The table is **round**.

Position of adjectives

Adjective usually comes **before** the noun it describes, but sometimes it can come **after** the noun (or a pronoun), later in the sentence.

Before a noun:

- Today is a **cold** day.

After a noun:

- He needs someone **talented** to do this job.

A **Circle the most suitable adjective in brackets for each sentence.**

1. The (blunt, sharp) knife should not be kept in open.

2. The (clean, dirty) road was being washed.

3. Raghu is a (brilliant, small) photographer.

4. He was (tired, thrilled) of listening to his boss's complaints.

5. She faced (ferocious, friendly) opposition from her critics.

6. He was praised for his (good, poor) marks in the exam.

POSSESSIVE ADJECTIVES

Possessive adjectives are the words that are used to *modify a noun* by showing *a form of possession or a sense of belonging* to a particular person or thing.

They are: **my, your, his, her, its, our and their.**

Examples:

- This is **my** room.

- Is that **your** car?

- This phone must be **his**.

- You must return **her** book before the exam.

- This is **our** car. **Their** car is red in colour.

A **Tick the correct word in the brackets in each sentence.**

1. He wants to get (his, her) certificate.

2. She showed (her, his) book to the class.

3. I was playing with (them, their) in the field.

4. My cousins are going back. I went to see (them, him) off.

5. We should keep (our, their) mobiles silent during the meeting.

6. The kitten was trying to find (its, her) mother.

7. I was having (my, your) lunch.

8. The drivers were parking (their, his) cars.

1. This mobile is his.

   _____

2. This book is not yours.

   _____

3. The new apartment is theirs.

   _____

4. The room is hers.

   _____

5. That bag is ours.

   _____

6. This bed is mine.

   _____

Other ways of showing possession

An **apostrophe** is normally **used** with the letter **'s'** to **show ownership** or **possession**. With most singular nouns, simply add an **apostrophe** plus the letter **'s'** to **do** this.

Example:

• This house belongs to Jatin.

   This is Jatin**'s** house.

• This car belongs to Nancy.

   This is Nancy**'s** car.

To make a **plural** noun **possessive**, simply add an **apostrophe** to the word. If the plural does not end in an **s,** then add an apostrophe plus **s.**

Examples:

- The boys' hostel

    (The hostel belonging to the boys)

- The Mittals' apartment.

    (The Mittals live in this apartment).

- The children's corner
  (Plural does not end in **s.**)

C **Use ('s) 0r (') with the words in the brackets to show possession.**

1. The _____ (pupils) belongings in the classroom were kept at a corner.

2. The _____ (women) husbands were opting for family insurance.

3. The _____ (ladies) hats are expensive.

4. The _____ (king) men rushed to welcome the prince.

5. The thieves ran away seeing _____ (policeman) gun.

6. The _____ (robber) fingerprints were found on the windshield.

7. The police checked the _____ (workers) passports.

8. I asked for this _____ (child) pen.

9. The storm raged the _____ (people) homes.

10. There is a wound on the _____ (girl) arm.

COMPARISON OF ADJECTIVES

Comparative degree of adjectives *are used to compare two nouns.*

Examples:

taller, bigger, slower, etc.

Superlative degree of adjectives *are used to compare three or more nouns.*

Examples:

tallest, biggest, slowest, etc.

Comparative adjectives

Comparative adjectives *compare one person or thing with another and enable us to say whether a person or thing has more or less of a particular quality:*

I am **taller than** you.

You are **more interested** in sports **than** studies.

We use the comparative with the word **than.**

Superlative adjectives

Superlative adjectives describe one person or thing as having more of a quality than all other people or things in a group:

This is **the tallest** building in India.

This is **the biggest** compliment I have ever got.

We use the superlative with the word **the.**

QUANTIFYING DETERMINERS

Adjectives that tell us about quantity are called *quantifying determiners, or adjectives of quantity. These words tell us how many people, animals, or things there are without specifying the exact amount or quantity.*

These are: **much, many, some, any, a few , lots of, plenty.**

Many and Much

Many is used with **countable nouns,** or plural nouns.

Examples:

- Kelvin does not have **many** friends.

- There are **many** empty chairs at the event.

- How **many** fruits are there on the table?

Much is used with **uncountable nouns** (which are often in singular form).

Examples:

- How **much** money have you got?

- This is what I get for drinking too **much** coffee.

- How **much** sleep do you get every night?

A Write 'much' or 'many' before the nouns below.

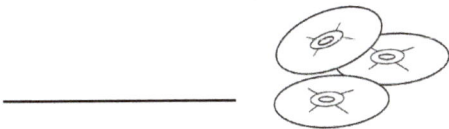

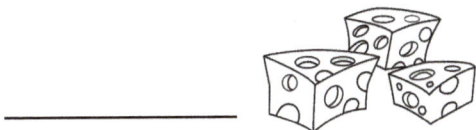

_____

_____

_____

_____

29

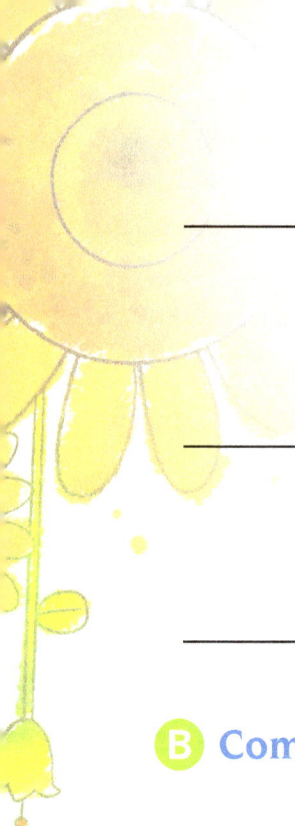

_____    _____

_____    _____

_____    _____

B **Complete the sentences below with 'much' or 'many'.**

1. How _____ orange juice is left?

2. There are _____ ants in the jar.

3. She puts too _____ sugar in the coffee.

4. How _____ flour did you buy?

5. Mother has not added _____ items to the shopping list.

6. There isn't _____ butter left.

7. How _____ times must I tell you to keep quiet?

8. Is there _____ time left before the game ends?

9. She invited _____ friends to her party.

10. There isn't _____ oil in the frying pan.

A LOT OF AND LOTS OF

A lot of and lots of are used to express that there is a *large quantity of something*. They both can be used in *positive sentences, negative sentences, and questions*.

They can be used with both **countable** or **uncountable nouns**.

'She has **a lot of** money ' can also be written as 'She has **lots of** money'.

Examples:

* There are **a lot of** dogs in the street.

* I have **a lot of** time to answer your questions.

* I saw **a lot of** people waiting in the queue.

* There are **lots of** people in the queue today.

* The teacher gave us **lots of** homework.

* We have **lots of** time to catch the plane; let's relax. (Uncountable noun)

A Fill in the blanks below with 'many','much' or 'a lot / lots of'.

1. There aren't _____ apples in the fridge.

2. There are _____ vegetables, but there isn't _____ fruit.

3. There isn't _____ water in your cup.

4. I have got _____ books in my library.

5. There isn't _____ sugar in her coffee.

6. Is there _____ pollution in Beijing?

FEW / A FEW AND LITTLE / A LITTLE

> *We use a **few** and a **little** to suggest a small quantity or not much of something.*

A few is used with **countable and plural nouns.**

A little is used with **uncountable nouns.**

Examples:

- There are only **a few** days left until Christmas.

- I have **a few** crazy friends.

- There's **a little** coffee left.

- There is **little** hope of finding your wallet.

While **Few** and **Little** usually have negative meanings (i.e. much less in quantity), especially when used with **very**.

- He is sad because he has **few** friends. (Countable noun)

- There are **few** honest politicians. (Countable noun)

- There is **little** hope of finding your wallet. (Uncountable noun)

- They have very **little** knowledge about politics. (Uncountable noun)

> **A few** is more in quantity than **few**; and **a little** is more in quantity than **little**.

A Complete each sentence with 'a few' or 'a little'.

1. I am donating _____ of my old clothes to charity.

2. Apply _____ cream to the wound.

32

3. Jenny could speak _____ Spanish after taking _____ lessons.

4. Could I have _____ milk in my coffee, please?

5. _____ monkeys escaped from the zoo yesterday.

6. Take _____ food even though you have no appetite.

7. The teacher gives us _____ time to prepare before a test.

8. There are only _____ days left to hand in the reports.

9. Knead _____ water into the dough to make it softer.

10. He speaks _____ French, so we were able to find a nice room in Paris.

11. He has only _____ coins left in his pocket.

12. I can see only _____ houses on the hill.

B Fill in the blanks below with 'a few' or 'a little'.

1. He died _____ months after his wife's death.

2. Please add _____ salt to the soup.

3. I can only see _____ houses on the hill.

4. I'm sorry, but I have _____ time to waste.

5. I have _____ interest in politics.

6. I am going cycling with _____ of my friends.

7. Let's leave her alone for _____ minutes.

SOME AND ANY

> Some *and* Any *may be used with both* countable *and* uncountable nouns.

Any is used **after not** and other negative words, as well as in **questions.**

Some is used in **positive sentences**.

Examples:

- Do we need **any** rice?

- **No,** we don't need **any** rice.

- We have **some** rice in the cupboard.

Some may also be used for **questions,** typically **offers** and **requests**, if we think the answer will be **positive**.

Examples:

- Would you like **some** coffee?

- Can I borrow **some** money?

A Use 'some' or 'any' to complete each sentence below.

1. I don't want _____ apples.

2. Can I have _____ coffee?

3. Are there _____ letters for me?

4. He does not have _____ patience.

5. Do you have _____ pets?

6. I can have _____ more tea, please.

VERBS

A verb is a word that expresses an action or a state of being.

Examples:

- He runs. **(action)**
- He is the president of America. **(state of being)**

Types of Verbs

A verb can be categorised as one of the following:

Action Verb

An action verb is a verb that conveys action.

Example:

- The dog **chases** the cat.
- A spider **spins** a web.

Action verbs are of two kinds:

1. Transitive Verb

A transitive verb is an action verb that acts on something (i.e., it has a direct object).

Example:

- He **writes** books.

(Here, the direct object is a book.)

- Lee **answers** all the questions.

(Here, the direct object is the **questions**.)

The direct object of a transitive verb can be found by finding the verb and asking "what?"

2. Intransitive Verb

An intransitive verb is an action verb that does not act on something (i.e., there is no direct object).

Example:

- The rain **fell.**

- My throat **hurts.**

Sometimes a preposition comes after an intransitive verb, followed by the object.

My friend **works** in (preposition) a bank (object).

John **lives** near (preposition) the stadium (object).

> Some verbs such as **meet, play sing, sleep, write** can be both **transitive and intransitive.**

Stative Verb

> **A stative verb** expresses a **state** rather than an action. A stative verb typically relates to a **state of being, a thought, or an emotion.**

Example:

- I **am** at home.

- She **believes** in fairies.

- He **feels** sad.

Auxiliary Verb

> **An auxiliary verb** (or helping verb) accompanies a **main verb** (action verb). It express either tense or voice. The most common auxiliary verbs are **be, do, and have** (in their various forms).

Examples:

- Harry **has** eaten all the candies.

(Here **has** helps to express **tense**.)

A Underline the correct word in the brackets in each sentence.

1. The cake you made yesterday (is, are, was) delicious.

2. If he (didn't, don't, doesn't) arrive on time, he'll have to take a later flight.

3. A spider (has, had, is) eight legs.

4. We (did, do, does) mental sums every day.

5. Good friends (do, does, are) things together.

6. Today I (had, has, have) $2 in my pocket.

7. Dad (had been, have been, has been) working hard all day.

8. There (were, was had) floods when the dam burst last year.

9. Sarah (don't, isn't, doesn't) ski or roller skate.

10. (Did, Has, Had) Sarah bring juice?

Modal Verb

A **modal verb** is a type of auxiliary verb used to express functions such as a**bility, possibility, permission, or an obligation.** The modal auxiliary verbs are **can, could, may, might, must, ought to, shall, should, will, and would.**

Examples:

- Harry **can** eat a lot of candies.
  (Here **can** helps to express *ability*.)

- Harry **might** eat that candy before he gets home.
  (Here **might** helps to express *possibility*.)

- Harry **may** eat as many candies as he likes.
  (Here *may* helps to express *permission*.)

We can't add -ing, -s or -ed to the modal verb.

B Fill in the blanks with appropriate modal auxiliary verbs.

1.   My grandmother is eighty-five, but she _____ still read and write without glasses.

2.   _____ I come with you?

3.   _____ you help me with the housework, please?

4.   There was a time when I _____ stay up very late.

5.   _____ I sit with you?

6.   You _____ stop when the traffic lights turn red.

7.   It is snowing outside so I _____ stay at home.

8.   I _____ get you a shawl from Kashmir.

9.   _____ you mind if I borrowed your car?

10.   _____ you take care of my dog for a day?

11.   I _____ to help mother with the housework.

12.   She _____ sell her home because she needs money.

ACTIVE VOICE AND PASSIVE VOICE

The voice of the verb represents the relationship between the action being described by it on the one hand, and the subject and the object on the other.

Active Voice

In active voice, the **subject performs the action**. He/she is the **doer** of the action.

> Subject (doer of the action) + Verb (action) + Object (receiver of the action)

Example:

- Some girls were helping the wounded woman.
- He played cricket.

The verb should be in accordance with the subject in the active voice.

Passive voice

In the **passive voice**, the **subject** is **not a doer**. The passive voice is used when we want to **emphasise the action (the verb) and the object** of a sentence rather than subject.

In passive voice, the sentence begins with the object, and the subject is at the end.

> Object (receiver of the action) + be (helping verb) + Main verb + by Subject (if any)

Example:

- The wounded woman **was being helped** by some girls.
- Cricket **was played** by him.

Read the following sentences:

- The glass **is broken**. (It is not important to know who broke the glass.)
- The class **has been cancelled**. (The focus is on the class being cancelled rather than who cancelled it.)
- The house **was built** in 2000. (It is not important to know who built the house.)

Changing from active voice to passive voice

The **object in the active sentence becomes a subject in the passive sentence.** The verb is changed to a "be" verb + past participle. The subject of the active sentence follows **by** or is omitted.

- Sam wrote a letter to Jamie.(active voice)
  A letter was written to Jamie by Sam. (passive voice)

- The government built a new bridge. (active voice)
  A new bridge was built by the government. (passive voice)

A Rewrite the following sentence in passive voice.

1. John gave me a bunch of flowers on my birthday.

   _____

2. The government has told the public a lot of lies.

   _____

3. The school governors gave the drama club quite a lot of money.

   _____

4. Peter drew this picture.

   _____

5. Anne arranges the flowers every week.

   _____

6. A Singapore company published this book.

   _____

7. Clouds hid the sun.

   _____

8. Mud covered me from head to toe.

   _____

9. Commuters crowd the platforms during rush hour.

   _____

10. The children have made all the decorations themselves.

    _____

There is a different way to change an active sentence that begins with people say, they say, everybody believes, some think, or nobody expects into a passive sentence.

Example:

- People thought that he was mad. (active voice)
  It was thought that he was mad./ He was thought to be mad. (passive voice)

- They appreciated your business. (active voice)
  Your business is appreciated. (passive voice)

ADVERBS

An **adverb** is a word that **describe a verb, an adjective, another adverb, a phrase, a clause, or a sentence.**

An **adverbial phrase** is an adverb that has **more than one word**. it usually starts with a preposition.

Example:

- I will sit here **silently**.

- I will stay here **in silence**.

Both the adverb **silently** and the adverbial phrase **in silence** describe the verb **sit**.

Types of adverb

Adverbs of Manner

An **adverb of manner** tells us how an action is carried out.

Example:

- He was sitting there **happily**.

- The dog barked **loudly**.

Very often, adverbs of manner are formed by adding **-ly or -ily** (in the words that end in **-y**) to the end of an adjective.

Example:

loud**ly**, slow**ly**, quick**ly**, heavi**ly**, etc.

Some adverbs of manner take the same spelling as the adjective and do not add an -ly to the end:

Example:

- He runs **fast**.

- They do their job **well**.

An **adverbial of place** is a phrase that is used as an **adverb of place.**

Examples:

- The book store is **over there**.

- There are potholes **all over the road**.

A **Fill in the blanks with an appropriate adverb of place from the clues given in the box.**

Wherever	downhill	abroad	nowhere	backwards	somewhere
outdoors	under	nearby	everywhere	upwards	

1. I have _____ to go.

2. I left my keys _____ in the house.

3. The game is meant to be played _____.

4. There is a grocery store _____.

5. The cat is hiding _____ the bed.

6. He fell _____.

7. _____ I go, I explore the local cuisine.

8. The lift is going _____.

9. NRI is the term for the Indian citizens who live _____.

10. Children like to play _____.

11. The skier went _____ at a high speed.

12. I looked _____ for my keys.

Adverbs of Time

Adverbs of time tell us **when** something happens. Adverbs of time are usually placed at the end of a sentence and answer the question **when?**.

Example:

- We visited my grandmother's house yesterday.

- The train is leaving soon.

B **Find out the adverbs of time in the given sentences and circle them.**

1. I visited my brother yesterday.

2. Rachel will go to her hometown tomorrow.

3. Kelvin completed his graduation last year.

4. I was roaming in the market all day.

5. The doctor is giving a talk this evening.

6. Today he woke up early.

7. I will visit my grandparents soon.

8. I got my salary yesterday.

9. I have to go now.

10. Saira forgot to bring her assignment today.

C **Underline the adverbs of time or place. Write in the brackets whether it shows when or where. The first one is done for you.**

1. "I want to go to the park <u>now</u>!" shouted Bill.   (**when**)

2. Your book is here.   ( )

3. We will go to the exhibition later.   (   )

4. I cannot find my keys anywhere.   (   )

5. Let's go somewhere this weekend.   (   )

6. We visited the orphanage yesterday.   (   )

7. My parents are touring Germany now.   (   )

8. There are flowers everywhere.   (   )

9. We will know the results of the test soon.   (   )

10. "Stay indoors. It's going to rain!" warned Mother.   (   )

Adverbs of Frequency

Adverbs of frequency are used to express time or **how often something happens.**

Example:

- It **never** snows in Singapore.

- I watch television **occasionally.**

D Underline the correct answer in the brackets.

1. The principal (often/ seldom) visits her pupil's homes. She only does so if it is absolutely necessary.

2. The postman delivers our mail (daily / often) except on Sundays and public holidays.

3. The lazy and naughty boy (rarely/ always) does his homework. His teacher complains to his parents all the time.

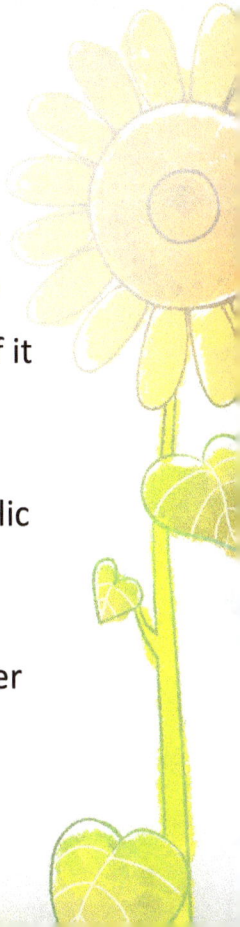

4. My mother is paid (daily/ monthly) on the last day of each month.

5. The Eskimos (always/ never)wear thin or light clothes as the temperature where they live is too cold.

E Choose the best options to complete each sentence.

1. It _____ snows in Toronto.

   (a) rarely   (b)often   (c) always   (d) seldom

2. Would you rather drive sometimes or take the train _____?

   (a) still   (b) never   (c) every day   (d) now

3. My brother is never sad. He is _____ happy.

   a) sometimes(b)always   (c) never   (d) seldom

4. I _____ read fiction books.

   a) rarely   (b)often   (c) always   (d) seldom

5. I _____ ride my bicycle.

   (a) never   (b) always   (c) sometimes   (d) often

6. My father _____ walks the dog.

   (a) always   (b) never   (c) often   (d) sometimes

Adverbs of Duration

An **adverb of duration** tells us for **how long** an action is done or **how long it lasts.**

Example:

- The phone was **temporarily** out of order.

- The H & M store is shifted **permanently** to a new address.

An **adverbial of duration** is a **phrase** that tells us for **how long** an action is done or **how long it lasts.**

Example:

- The phone is switched off **for the time being.**

- The journal is published **once a month.**

F **Fill in the blanks with an adverb (or adverbial) of duration.**

1.   Agnes stayed _____ at her cousin's house.

2.   We didn't stay _____ at the meeting.

3.   He will_____ be her little boy.

4.   We spoke _____.

5.   I will be _____ grateful.

PREPOSITION

A **preposition** is a **word** or a **set of words** that are used to link a **person, place, animal or thing** to other words within the sentence.

It tells us if the words are related by **place, direction, time, or manner.**

Example:

- Place: The book is **on** the table.

- Direction: She walked **towards** the door.

- Time: I will meet you **after** 5 pm.

- Manner: He spoke **with** confidence.

Types of prepositions

1. **Preposition of place (spatial)**
   These prepositions are used to illustrate the location of nouns or **pronouns** in a sentence.

   Example: In, On, Between, Behind, Under, Over, Near, etc.

2. **Preposition for direction** These are used to describe the movement of one noun or pronoun towards another noun or pronoun.

   Example: to, into, towards, through, etc.

3. **Preposition of time** These are used when there is a need to indicate when a particular event happened.

   Example: In, On, At, Since, For, During, etc.

4. **Preposition for manner** These are applied to describe the way or means by which something happened or happens, when used in a sentence.

   Example: On, In, With, By, Like, etc.

CONJUNCTIONS

A **conjunction** is a **joining word.** It connects **words or groups of words.**

Conjunctions are also called **connectors.** Some **connectors** are : **and, or, but, as well as, both, not only... but also etc.**

Example:

- I like coffee, **but** I don't like tea.

- She is smart **and** beautiful.

- He is **not only** tall, **but also** good at basketball.

- I will go to the store, **or** I will stay home.

Types of conjunctions

There are **three basic types of conjunctions:**

1. **coordinating conjunctions**

2. **subordinating conjunctions**

3. **correlative conjunctions.**

Coordinating conjunctions

It shows that the **parts of the sentence that it connects are of equal importance.** Some coordinating conjunctions include **and, but, or, not, for, so , yet, because, etc.**

Example:

- I like coffee **and** tea.

- I will go to the store **or** stay home.

- She is smart **but** not beautiful.

- He is tall **so** he can reach the top shelf.

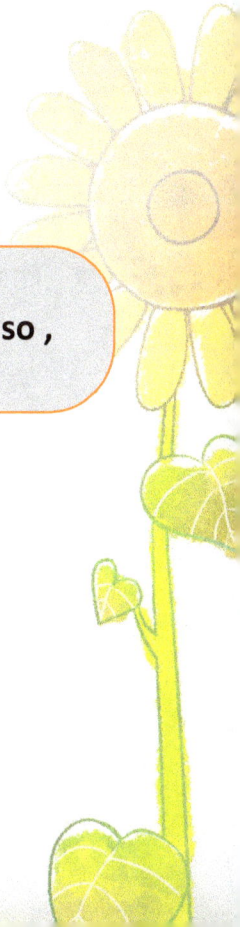

Subordinating conjunctions

It shows that **one part of a sentence is dependent on another.** The part that is dependent is introduced by conjunctions such as **when, while, where, whereas, since, so that, as, than, if, even, though, before, after, etc.**

Example:

* I went to bed early **because** I was tired.

* **Whereas** I like coffee, my sister likes tea.

* I was reading a book **while** my sister was watching TV.

* I kept on working **even** when I was sick.

Correlative conjunctions

Correlative conjunctions also connect sentences of equal importance, but **they work in pairs.** They include pairs such as **either...or, neither...nor, not only...but also, both.... also, such... that, etc.**

Example:

* **Either** you come with me **or** you stay here.

* **Neither** the teacher **nor** the students were happy with the result.

* **Not only** did he finish his homework **but also** he studied for the test.

* The boy asked **such** a foolish question **that** everybody laughed at him.

PUNCTUATION

> Punctuation *is a set of marks that help to* structure and organise different texts. *It is used to create sense, clarity, and stress in sentences.*

The most common punctuation marks in English are: **capital letters and full stops, question marks, commas, colons and semi-colons, exclamation marks and quotation marks.**

Capital Letters

> **Capital letters** are used to **mark the beginning of a sentence.**

Example:

We went to London last summer. **W**e stayed with my aunt, who lives there.

Capital letters are used at the **beginning of proper nouns,** which include **personal names (including titles before names), nationalities, and languages, days of the week and months of the year, public holidays, as well as geographical places.**

Example:

*   **D**r. **D**avid **J**ames is the consultant at **L**eeds **C**ity **H**ospital in **W**est **Y**orkshire.

*   He is an **E**nglishman but speaks **G**erman and **S**panish too.

*   We will again meet on **M**onday.

*   How are you celebrating **C**hristmas this year?

Capital letters are used for the **titles of books, magazines and newspapers, plays and music.**

Examples:

*   **T**he **L**ord of the **R**ings is a film series of three epic fantasy adventure films.

*   '**O**liver' is a musical based on the novel '**O**liver **T**wist' by Charles Dickens.

*   The **W**all **S**treet **J**ournal is America's largest newspaper.

The Full Stop (.)

The **full stop** or period **marks the end of a statement, a mild command or an indirect question.**

Example:

- The Yarlung Tsangpo is regarded as the highest river in the world**.** (statement)

- Shut the door. (command)

- My aunt asked me why I was sad. (Indirect question)

In addition to closing sentences, we also use **full stops in initials for personal names.**

Example:

- S.K. Woolworth

- J.K. Rowling

The Question Mark (?)

We place a **question mark** at the **end of a direct question.**

Example:

- Did you sleep well last night**?**

- Where are you going**?**

Exclamation marks (!)

Exclamation marks are used at the end of sentences.

(a) to show strong feelings such as **joy, surprise, and anger.**

Example:

- Mother came in and said," It's dinner time**!**"

- What a delicious cake**!**

(b) that give orders.

Example:

- Get out of my sight**!**

- Put the phone down**!**

Commas (,)

Commas are used (a) **to separate a list of similar words or phrases.**

Example:

- I have never met a more humble**,** more submissive**,** more respectful person than him.

- It is very important to write in clear**,** simple, and accurate words.

(b) in a **series of places or items** (except before the last place or item in the series where we use **and**).

Example:

- They travelled through Italy, Austria, the Czech Republic, **and** Poland.

- There are apples, oranges, grapes, **and** pears in the basket.

(c) to **pause slightly** in a **long sentence:**

Example:

- When mother went to the market this morning to buy groceries, she met her old childhood friend.

- James, our guide, will accompany you on the boat across to the island.

(d) in a direct address.

Example:

- We could not have done it without you, Lisa.

- Mother, can we leave now?

(e) in **dates.**

- He was born on Tuesday, January 27, 1998.

- On June 10, 2019, Tropical Cyclone VAYU formed over the eastern Arabian Sea (Indian Ocean) and started moving north.

(f) after **yes** or **no.**

- Yes, he is my younger brother.

- No, I cannot come today.

(g) before **please** if it comes **at the end of the sentence.**

- Could you wash the dishes, please?

- Don't forget to lock the door, please.

(h) to **set off quoted words.**

- "I think it is a great idea", said Clark.

- "Yes", said Mother.

Colons (:) and Semi-colons (;)

Colons are used

(a) to **introduce lists:**

- For the basic singing lesson, you will learn: breathing techniques, rhythm, harmony, voice control, and voice presentation.

(b) to **introduce the words spoken by people in a play.**

Example:

- Penny: What a beautiful day!

- Sara: Shall we go to the beach for a picnic?

(c) between sentences when the **second sentence explains or justifies the first sentence:**

Example:

- The park had been unused for some time: it was full of rotting trees and overgrown weeds.

- Keep your apartment neat and clean: it will attract more buyers.

Semi-colons are used instead of full stops to **separate two main clauses.** In such cases, the clauses are related in meaning but are separated grammatically:

Spanish is spoken throughout South America; in Brazil, the main language is Portuguese.

Quotation marks ('...' or "...")

Quotation marks are used in pairs to **set off direct speech, a quotation, or a phrase.**

Example:

- Ali said, "Where can we find a nice Mexican restaurant?"

- "Why don't they know who is responsible?" they asked.

- My grandmother always said, "A penny saved is a penny earned."

Ⓐ **Rewrite the following sentences using appropriate punctuation marks and capital letters wherever necessary.**

1. i know the names of the chinese boys in my class they are alan tan lee kah cheng and goh kok keng

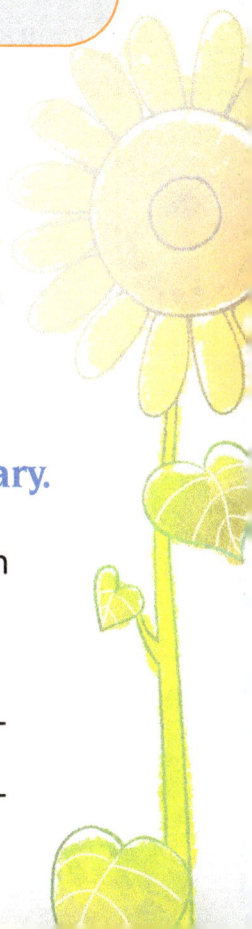

_____

_____

SENTENCES

A sentence *is a word or a group of words that* makes complete sense.

A sentence begins with a capital letter and ends with a full-stop, a question mark, or an exclamation mark.

Example:

- He is a good boy**.** (statement)

- Is he a good boy**?** (question)

- What a nice weather**!** (exclamation)

Types of Sentence

There are four types of sentences.

a. A declarative sentence: A declarative sentence **states a fact** and **ends with a full stop(.)** .

Example:

- Miss Peterson is a good teacher.

- Roger was the first one to reach the finish line.

b. An imperative sentence: An imperative sentence is a **command or a polite request**. It **ends with an exclamation mark(!) or a full stop(.).**

Example:

- Come here**!**

- Please play the movie**.**

c. An exclamatory sentence: An exclamatory sentence expresses **excitement or emotion**. It **ends** with an **exclamation mark(!)**.

Example:

- Wow! That was such an exciting movie**!**

- What a delicious cake**!**

d. An interrogative sentence: An interrogative sentence asks a **question** and ends with a question mark.

Example:

- Would you like to have tea or coffee**?**
- Have you got an atlas**?**

A **Identify the type of sentences.**

1. Music is my passion.

   _____

2. Have some mercy upon us.

   _____

3. How hot the day is!

   _____

4. Why are you sitting alone?

   _____

5. Please be quiet.

   _____

6. This is not my cup of tea.

   _____

7. What a beautiful painting!

   _____

8. Where do you live?

   _____

Structure of a sentence

Ideally, a **sentence** requires at least one **subject** and one **verb**. Sometimes the subject of a sentence can be hidden, but the verb must be visible and present in the sentence.

In simple terms, a **sentence** is a set of words that contain:

1. a **subject** (the person or thing we are talking about), and

2. a **predicate** (tells something about the subject)

Example:

* You speak English.

Here **you** is the **subject**,

and **speak English** is the **predicate**.

(speak is the **verb).**

* The Sun shines during the day.

Here **The Sun** is the **subject**,

and **shines during the day** is the **predicate.**

(shines is the **verb).**

B Read each sentence below and identify the subject and predicate. Write them in the table. The first one is done for you.

1. The teacher teaches well.
2. Stars twinkle at night.
3. Flowers bloom in the garden.
4. Dogs like to bark and sniff.
5. Active boys never stop playing.
6. The birds always sing early in the morning.
7. The horse is white.
8. The young pilot reads the storm warning.
9. Taylor and Charlie played with their toys.
10. The waiter tripped and fell over the diner's legs.

Subject	Predicate
The teacher	teaches well

ANSWER KEY

Noun

(A)

1. Common noun
2. Proper Noun
3. Proper Noun
4. Common noun, Common noun
5. Common noun
6. Proper Noun, Common Noun
7. Proper Noun, Proper Noun
8. Common noun , Common noun

Collective Nouns

(A)

1. choir
2. swarm

Abstract Nouns

(A)

1. chilhood, love and happiness
2. peace
3. fun
4. sight and smell
5. pride
6. anger
7. nightmare
8. patriotism
9. wisdom
10. luck

Other Types of Nouns

(A)

1. Widow
2. Bride
3. Grand-mother
4. Saleswoman
5. Bitch
6. Geese
7. Goddess
8. Mistress
9. Huntress
10. Benefactress
11. Empress
12. Governess

Articles

(A)

1. a **and** the
2. the
3. an
4. a

5. a
6. the
7. the **and** the
8. an
9. the
10. a

(B)

1. an **and** a
2. the
3. the
4. a
5. An
6. A **and** the
7. The
8. a
9. the
10. An **and** an

(C)

1. **a**
2. the

Pronoun

(A)

My family consists of four people: my parents, my sister, and me. **They** are very supportive and loving. My father works as a doctor and **he** enjoys reading books in **his** spare time. My mother is a teacher and **she** likes to cook delicious meals for **us**. My sister is a student and **she** loves to play the piano.

(B)

1. Taj Mahal
2. Dad and I

(C)

1. his
2. theirs
3. hers
4. ours
5. yours
6. mine
7. his
8. theirs

(D)

1. whom
2. who
3. whomever
4. where
5. that
6. whose

7. which
8. that
9. when
10. where

(E)

1. These
2. that
3. those
4. this
5. these
6. that
7. These **and** those
8. This **and** that

(F)

1. Who
2. Whose
3. What
4. Which
5. Who
6. Whom
7. What
8. Whose

(G)

1. herself
2. yourselves
3. itself
4. yourself
5. himself
6. myself
7. herself
8. ourselves
9. themselves
10. herself

Adjectives

(A)

1. sharp
2. dirty
3. brilliant
4. tired
5. ferocious
6. good

Possessive Adjectives

(A)

1. his
2. her
3. them
4. them
5. our
6. Its
7. my
8. their

(B)

1. This is his mobile.
2. This is not your book.

3. This is their new apartment.
4. This is her room.
5. These are our bags.
6. This is my bed.

(C)

1. .pupils'
2. women's
3. ladies'
4. king's
5. policeman's
6. robber's
7. workers'
8. child's
9. people's
10. girl's

Quantifying Determiners

(A)

many	CDs
many	pencils
much	cheese
much	music
many	cornflakes
many	cups
much	juice
many	pizzas
much	lemonade
much	time

(B)

1. much
2. many
3. much
4. much
5. many
6. much
7. many
8. much
9. many
10. much

A lot of and lots of

(A)

1. many
2. a lot of **and** much
3. much
4. a lot of
5. much
6. a lot of

Few/ A few and Little/ A little

(A)

1. A few
2. a little
3. a little **and** a few
4. a little

5. a few
6. a little
7. a little
8. a few
9. a little
10. a little
11. a few
12. a few

(B)

1. A few
2. a little
3. a few
4. little
5. little
6. a few
7. a few

Some and Any

(A)

1. any
2. some
3. any
4. any
5. any
6. some

Verbs

(A)

1. was
2. doesn't
3. has
4. do
5. do
6. have
7. has been
8. were
9. doesn't
10. Did

(B)

1. can
2. can
3. could
4. could
5. may
6. must
7. will
8. will
9. would
10. will
11. ought
12. might

Active Voice and Passive Voice

(A)

1. I was given a bunch of flowers on my birthday by John.
2. The public have been told a lot of lies by the

government.
3. The drama club was given quite a lot of money by the school governors.
4. The picture was drawn by Peter.
5. The flowers were arranged every week by Anne.
6. This book was published by a Singapore company.
7. The sun was hidden by clouds.
8. I was covered in mud from head to toe.
9. The platforms were crowded by commuters during rush hour.
10. All the decorations have been made by the children themselves.

Adverbs

(A)

1. nowhere
2. somewhere
3. outdoors
4. nearby
5. under
6. backwards
7. Wherever
8. upwards
9. abroad
10. outdoors
11. downhill
12. everywhere

(B)

1. yesterday
2. tomorrow
3. last year
4. all day
5. this evening
6. early
7. soon
8. yesterday
9. now
10. today

(C)

1. when
2. where
3. when
4. where
5. where
6. when
7. when
8. where
9. when
10. where

(D)

1. seldom
2. daily
3. rarely
4. monthly
5. never

(E)

1. often
2. everyday
3. always
4. rarely
5. sometimes
6. often

(F)

1. overnight
2. long
3. forever
4. briefly
5. forever

Punctuation

(A)

1. I know the names of the Chinese boys in my class. They are Alan Tan, Lee Kah Cheng and Goh Kok Keng.

Sentences

(A)

1. Declarative sentence
2. Imperative sentence
3. Exclamatory sentence
4. Interrogative sentence
5. Imperative sentence
6. Declarative sentence
7. Exclamatory sentence
8. Interrogative sentence

(B)

Subject	Predicate
The teacher	teaches well
Stars	twinkle at night
Flowers	bloom in the garden
Dogs	like to bark and sniff
Active boys	never stop playing
The birds	always sing early in the morning
The horse	is white
The young pilot	reads the storm warning
Taylor and Charlie	played with their toys
The waiter	tripped and fell over the diner's legs

www.ingramcontent.com/pod-product-compliance
Lightning Source LLC
LaVergne TN
LVHW081336060426

835513LV00014B/1317